The Emperor's Nightingale

and other magical stories

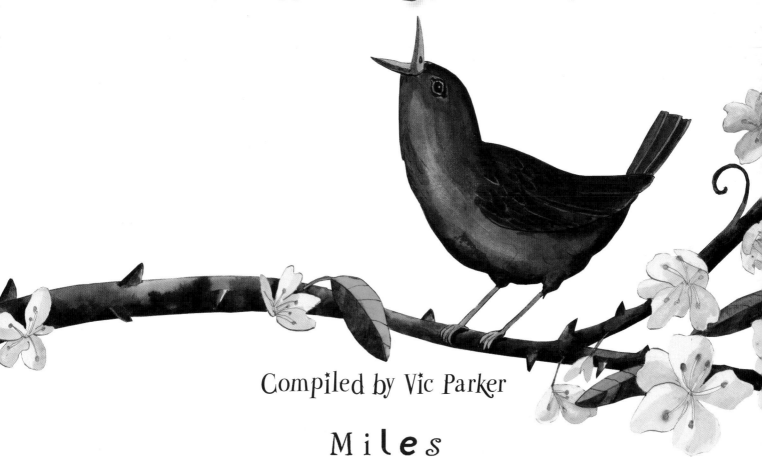

Compiled by Vic Parker

Miles Kelly

First published in 2012 by Miles Kelly Publishing Ltd
Harding's Barn, Bardfield End Green, Thaxted, Essex, CM6 3PX, UK

Copyright © Miles Kelly Publishing Ltd 2011

2 4 6 8 10 9 7 5 3 1

Publishing Director Belinda Gallagher
Creative Director Jo Cowan
Editorial Director Rosie McGuire
Editor Carly Blake
Senior Designer Joe Jones
Editorial Assistant Lauren White
Production Manager Elizabeth Collins
Reprographics Anthony Cambray, Stephan Davis, Jennifer Hunt

ISBN 978-1-84810-576-8

Printed in China

British Library Cataloguing-in-Publication Data
A catalogue record for this book is available from the British Library

ACKNOWLEDGEMENTS

The publishers would like to thank the following artists who have contributed to this book:
Cover: Peter Cottrill at The Bright Agency
Advocate Art: Alida Massari
The Bright Agency: Marcin Piwowarski, Tom Sperling
Marsela Hajdinjak

All other artwork from the Miles Kelly Artwork Bank

The publishers would like to thank the following sources for the use of their photographs:
Shutterstock: (page decorations) Dragana Francuski Tolimir
Dreamstime: (frames) Gordan

Every effort has been made to acknowledge the source and copyright holder of each picture.
Miles Kelly Publishing apologises for any unintentional errors or omissions.

Made with paper from a sustainable forest

www.mileskelly.net   info@mileskelly.net

www.factsforprojects.com

Contents

The Mermaid and the Boy   4

The Emperor's Nightingale   15

The Frog   26

The Half-Chick   34

The Mermaid and the Boy

From Andrew Lang's *Brown Fairy Book*

LONG AGO, there lived a king who ruled over a country by the sea. Once, he had to leave his wife to visit his subjects in some distant islands. The king set off on the long sea voyage, but his ship soon ran upon a rock, and was stuck fast.

Suddenly a mermaid was seen dancing on the waves which threatened every moment to dash the ship to pieces. "There is only

4

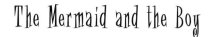

one way to free yourselves," she said to the king, "and that is to give me your solemn word that you will deliver to me the first child that is born to you."

Just then a huge wave broke with great force on the ship's side, and the king's crew fell on their knees and begged him to save them.

So he promised, and this time a wave lifted the vessel clean off the rocks, into the open sea.

In the fullness of time, a year after the king had returned home, he was overjoyed when the queen gave birth to a baby boy. But from that moment, he and the queen lived in terror, wondering if their son was to be snatched away.

When the prince was sixteen, the king and his wife decided that for his own sake, it would be best to send him into the world, for then perhaps the mermaid would never find him. The prince was delighted at the thought of adventures.

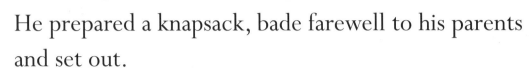

He prepared a knapsack, bade farewell to his parents and set out.

All day he walked, till evening drew in. He was just about to stretch himself out on a soft mossy bank under a tree, when there was a fearful roar and a lion stood before him.

"Give me some food," said the lion, "it is past my supper time, and I am very hungry."

The boy was so thankful that the lion did not want to eat him, that he gladly picked up his knapsack and held out some bread and a flask of wine.

"I must be off now," remarked the lion, when he was done, "but if you are in any danger just wish yourself a lion and you will become one on the spot. One good turn deserves another, you know."

The prince thanked him for his kindness, and the two then bade each other farewell.

Next day, the boy again walked until evening drew in. Then he prepared a sleeping place in some ferns. Suddenly there was a crashing noise and the boy saw a huge black bear thundering towards him.

"I am hungry," cried the bear. "Give me something to eat."

From his knapsack the prince took out his second flask of wine and another loaf of bread.

"I must go now," said the bear, when he was done, "but when you are in any danger just wish yourself a bear and you will become one. One good turn deserves another, you know."

And the boy and the bear bade each other farewell.

On the third day, the prince once again walked until evening drew in, whereupon he threw himself down under a tree to rest. Then, he heard a great buzzing over his head.

"I am hungry," said a bee in a cross voice. "Give me something to eat."

The boy took his last loaf and flask out of his knapsack and laid them on the ground, and they had supper together.

"I must be off," said the bee when he was done. "But if you are in danger just wish yourself a bee and you will become one. One good turn deserves another, you know." And the bee departed.

Next day, the boy walked and walked until he entered a great city. He listened to the people gossiping and heard much talk about the king's only daughter, who was extremely beautiful.

The prince waited until everyone had gone to bed, then he wished himself a bee, and flew through the keyhole in the front door of the palace, up the great stairs, past the guards, and through the keyhole into the princess's chamber. Then he turned into a man again.

The princess, who was awake, was so startled that she couldn't even scream – she just sat up in bed gazing at him in silent terror.

8

"Do not be afraid," he said, "I shall not hurt you." And he began to praise her gardens, of which he had also heard the people speak, and the birds and flowers which she loved, till the princess's anger softened, and she answered him with gentle words. Indeed, she was so charmed by the prince that she vowed she would marry him, and confided to him that in three days her father would be off to the wars, leaving his sword in her room. If any man could find it and bring it to him he would receive her hand as a reward.

At this point the youth jumped up hastily saying: "Of course I shall ride with the king to the war, and if I do not return, take your violin every evening to the seashore and play on it."

Just as the princess had foretold, in three days the king set out for the war with a large following, and among them was the young prince. They had left the city many miles behind them, when the king suddenly discovered that he had forgotten his sword, and though each and every one of his attendants immediately offered theirs, he declared that he could fight with none but his own.

"The first man who brings it to me from my daughter's room," cried he, "shall not only have her to wife, but after my death shall reign in my stead."

At this the young prince, a Red Knight and several more turned their horses to ride as fast as the wind back to the palace. But suddenly a better plan entered the prince's head, and, letting the others pass him, he wished himself a lion. Then on he bounded, uttering such dreadful roars that the horses were frightened and grew unmanageable, and he easily outstripped them, and soon reached the gates of the palace. Here he hastily changed himself into a bee, and flew straight into the princess's room, where he became a man again. She showed him where the sword hung concealed behind a curtain, and he took it down, saying as he did so: "Be sure not to forget what you have promised to do."

The princess made no reply, but smiled sweetly, and slipping a golden ring from her finger she broke it in two and held half out to the prince, while the other half she put in her pocket. He kissed it, and ran down the stairs with the sword.

On his way back to the king, he stopped at a stream. Unbuckling the sword, he flung himself on the ground for a long drink. Unluckily, the mermaid happened at that moment to be floating on the water not very far off, and knew he was the boy who had been given her before he was born. So she floated gently up, seized his arm, and the waves closed over them both. Hardly had they disappeared, when the Red Knight came by – he could scarcely believe his eyes when he saw the king's sword on the bank. He fastened it to his belt and carried it off to the king.

When the war was over and the king and his

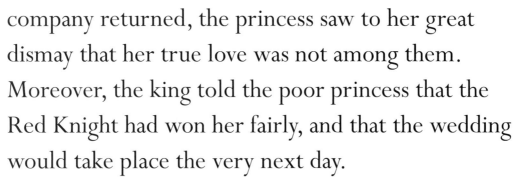

company returned, the princess saw to her great dismay that her true love was not among them. Moreover, the king told the poor princess that the Red Knight had won her fairly, and that the wedding would take place the very next day.

That evening, taking her violin under her arm, the princess crept down to the shore as she had promised.

"Listen!" said the mermaid to the prince, who was lying stretched on a bed of seaweeds at the bottom of the sea. "Listen! That is your old love playing."

"I hear nothing," answered the youth, who did not look happy. "Take me up higher, where the sounds can reach me."

So the mermaid took him on her shoulders and bore him right up to the surface. "Can you hear now?" she asked.

As soon as the prince thrust his head and shoulders into the air, he wished himself a bee, and flew straight into the pocket of the princess. The mermaid looked in vain for him all night, but he never came back, and never more did he gladden her eyes.

But the princess felt that something strange was about her, and returned quickly to the palace, where the young man at once resumed his own shape. Oh, what joy filled her heart at the sight of him! But there was no time to be lost, and she led him right into the great hall, where the king and his nobles were sitting feasting.

"Behold the gallant prince who fetched your sword by the powers of his great magic!" the princess announced. To prove it, the prince turned himself into a lion, and the Red Knight quaked with fear. Then the prince turned himself into a bear, and the Red Knight hid behind the princess. Then the prince turned himself into a bee, and stung the Red Knight repeatedly until he fled the palace, never to be seen again.

How the king and his nobles laughed with joy!

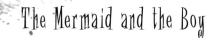

The princess drew out her half of the golden ring and showed how it fitted the prince's half perfectly. And next day, there was indeed a marriage feast for the princess and her true prince.

The Emperor's Nightingale

From *Tales of Wonder Every Child Should Know*
by Kate Douglas Wiggin and Nora Archibald Smith

THE EMPEROR OF CHINA lived in the most beautiful palace in the world, surrounded by such a beautiful, large garden that the gardener himself did not quite know where it ended. If you kept on far enough, you came to a mighty forest which stretched down so close to the sea that the poor fishermen in their boats could sail under the overhanging branches.

In one of these boughs a nightingale lived, and so beautiful was its song that the sailors would stop to listen on their way out to spread their nets.

"Heavens! How gloriously that bird sings!" they would exclaim.

Travellers came from all over the world to see the emperor's city and his palace and garden, but when they heard the nightingale, they would say: "That is most beautiful of all." And when the travellers reached their homes again, they told all their friends of the wonderful things they had seen and heard, and wise people wrote books, in which they did not forget to tell of the nightingale. Even the poets wrote verses about this nightingale that lived in the wood by the sea.

And then, one by one, the books travelled all over the world, until some at last reached the hands of the emperor, who sat in his golden chair and read them, nodding his head with pleasure, for he was charmed with the beautiful descriptions of his city and castle and garden. Then he read the words: 'The nightingale is the most lovely thing of all!'

"What is this?" he said. "The nightingale!

I have never heard of such a bird, yet there seems to be one in my empire – and in my own garden! Imagine learning of such a thing for the first time from a book!"

Thereupon he summoned his chamberlain to find the bird.

"I must hear the nightingale," the emperor demanded. "I command it to perform for me this evening."

The chamberlain raced up and down stairs and through all the corridors again, accompanied by half the court, all searching for the nightingale.

At length they came to the kitchen, where a poor little scullery-maid at once exclaimed: "Why, yes, I know it well – and it sings beautifully!"

So the girl led the chamberlain and all the court into the wood.

"Listen!" said the girl. "There it sits up in the branches," and she pointed to a tiny bird clinging to a spray of thorn.

"I should never have believed it would look like that," exclaimed the chamberlain. "It looks so simple and so pale, it must be frightened at the sight of so many grand people."

"Dear nightingale," called the little girl, "our most noble emperor desires you to sing to him."

"Oh, certainly, with pleasure," promised the nightingale, and accompanied everyone back through the wood.

When the little bird began to sing in the splendid palace, he sang so gloriously that the emperor's eyes filled with tears which overflowed and ran down his cheeks. The emperor was so delighted that he commanded the nightingale to live at court, in its own cage, with permission to fly out twice a day, and once during the night. On these trips it was accompanied by twelve servants, each of whom held a silken cord attached to its leg, so that really there could not be the slightest pleasure for it in such a flight. As for the city, wherever you went, you met

people talking of the wonderful bird, and news of it spread even further than before.

One day a gift arrived at the palace, addressed to the emperor, with the words: 'A nightingale from the Emperor of Japan' written on the outside of the casket.

A wonderful work of art lay within, a clockwork nightingale, encrusted in diamonds and rubies and pearls, and fashioned in the shape of a real bird. When it had been wound up it sang, and its glittering tail moved up and down in time to the notes. A ribbon hung around its neck, and on it these words were written: 'The Emperor of Japan's nightingale is nothing compared to that of the Emperor of China'.

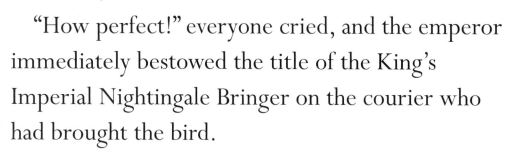

"How perfect!" everyone cried, and the emperor immediately bestowed the title of the King's Imperial Nightingale Bringer on the courier who had brought the bird.

"Now we must hear them sing a duet together. How beautiful it will sound!" they all said. But it did not sound so well as they had expected, for the real bird sang in a natural way, and just whatever came into its little throat, and the artificial bird could only sing a waltz.

So then the new one had to sing by itself and obtained quite as much applause as the real one had done. Besides, it looked so much handsomer, glittering and gleaming like bracelets and breast-pins.

Over and over again, for quite thirty-three times, it sang the same tune and yet was not tired. The courtiers would have liked to hear it again even, only the emperor said, "No, it's the real bird's turn now, let us ask it to sing."

But where was the nightingale? Not a soul had

seen it fly out of the open window back to its own green woods.

"Well, well! Whatever has become of it?" exclaimed the emperor. And all the courtiers united in saying it was a most ungrateful creature.

"After all," they said, "we still have the better bird," and with that the new one had to sing his song for the thirty-fourth time.

And so the real nightingale was sent into exile, and the imitation one slept on a satin cushion very close to the emperor's bed. All the jewels and precious stones that had been showered on it as presents were arranged around the edge of the cushion, and it was given the title of the Emperor's Own Court Singer.

A whole year passed by in this fashion, and at last the emperor and his court and all the Chinese people knew every turn and trill of the nightingale's song by heart.

One evening the emperor lay in his bed listening

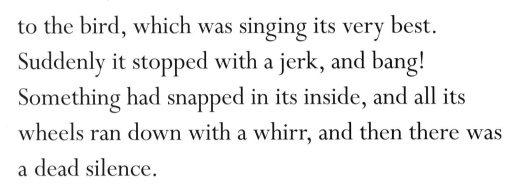

to the bird, which was singing its very best. Suddenly it stopped with a jerk, and bang! Something had snapped in its inside, and all its wheels ran down with a whirr, and then there was a dead silence.

The emperor sprang out of bed and sent for the court physician, but he could do nothing. Then a watchmaker was fetched, and after he had talked a lot, and examined the inside a great deal, he was able to put it in something like working order again.

"You must not use it too much," he said, "it is nearly worn out, and one can never put in fresh works again and be sure of the music being as good as before."

At this there was great mourning all over the country, for the imitation bird must only be allowed to sing once a year in future, and even that might prove too much for it.

After five years had passed the emperor fell very ill. All the people felt sad, for they were really extremely fond of him, and now it was said he could not possibly live.

White and cold the old emperor lay in his great tall bed, and all the courtiers thought he was dead, and ran away to greet their new king. But the emperor was yet alive – though barely. He lay still upon the magnificent bed, with its heavy velvet draperies and gorgeous golden tassels. High up, through the open window, the moon shone in upon him and the imitation nightingale lay in its casket by the bed.

A terrible weight seemed pressing on the emperor's chest, and he opened his eyes to see Death himself sitting there before him, whispering to him to come.

"Music! I want music! So I cannot hear the call of Death," gasped the emperor. But the imitation bird was silent, for until someone wound it up, it could not sing, and there was no one to do it. And Death still sat gazing at him with hollow, hungry eyes.

Suddenly a silvery note floated in at the open window. It was the voice of the real nightingale as it sat upon a bough outside. It had heard the emperor was ill, and had come back to comfort him and fill him with hope.

And as its song gained strength and rose and fell in delicious trills, the warm life blood began to flow anew in the emperor's veins, and Death was filled with a yearning to be in his own garden, and passed like a grey mist out of the open window.

"Deep, deep thanks I give you," said the emperor. "Merciful little bird! It was you I banished from my presence and my kingdom. And yet, you have charmed Death from my heart! You must never leave me – but you shall only sing when you desire, and I will break the artificial bird into a million pieces."

"No, spare it," said the nightingale. "It did its best as long as it was able, so keep it as before. I cannot build my nest within the castle, but I will often

come to you at evening and sing, on the bough outside the window, songs that will make you glad."

So saying the nightingale flew away.

Then the servants entered to attend to their dead emperor, and when they saw him standing there strong and well, they started back, aghast.

But the emperor only said: "Good morning!"

The Frog

From Andrew Lang's *Violet Fairy Book*

ONCE UPON A TIME there was a woman who had three sons. They were farmers, and the soil on which they lived was fruitful, and yielded rich crops. One day they all three told their mother they meant to get married. To which their mother replied: "Do as you like, but see that you choose good housewives – and, to make certain of this, take these three skeins of flax, and give it to them to spin. Whoever spins the best will be my favourite daughter-in-law."

Now the two eldest sons had already chosen

their wives, so they took the flax and carried it off with them, to have it spun as she had said. But the youngest son was puzzled what to do with his skein, as he knew no girl to whom he could give it to be spun. He wandered hither and thither, asking the girls that he met if they would undertake the task, but none would do so. Then he went out into the country and, seating himself on the bank of a pond, began to cry bitterly.

Suddenly there was a noise close beside him, and a frog jumped out of the water and asked him why he was crying. The youth told her of his trouble, and the frog said: "Do not weep. Give me the thread, and I will spin it for you." And, having said this, she took it out of his hand, and flopped back into the water, and the youth went back, not knowing what would happen next.

In a short time the two elder brothers came home, bringing with them the linen that had been spun by their chosen wives to show their mother. But the youngest brother was greatly troubled, for he had nothing to show. Sadly he took himself to the pond and, sitting down on the bank, began to weep.

Flop! And the frog appeared out of the water close beside him.

"Take this," she said, "here is the linen that I have spun for you."

You may imagine how delighted the youth was. He took the linen straight back to his mother, who declared she had never seen linen so beautifully spun. Indeed, she said it was far finer and whiter than the webs that the two elder brothers had brought home.

Then she turned to her sons and said: "But this is not enough, my sons, I must have another proof as to what sort of wives you have chosen. In the house there are three puppies. Each of you take one, and give it to the woman whom you mean to bring home as your wife. She must train it and bring it up.

Whichever dog turns out the best, its mistress will be my favourite daughter-in-law."

So the young men set out on their different ways, each taking a puppy with him. The youngest, not knowing where to go, returned to the pond, sat down once more on the bank, and began to weep.

Flop! And close beside him, he saw the frog. "Why are you weeping?" she said. Then he told her his difficulty, and that he did not know to whom he should take the puppy. "Give it to me," she said, "and I will bring it up for you." And she took the little creature out of his arms and disappeared with it into the pond.

The weeks and months passed, till one day the mother said she would like to see how the dogs had been trained by her future daughters-in-law. The two eldest sons departed, and returned shortly, leading with them two great mastiffs, who growled so fiercely, and looked so savage, that the mere sight of them made the mother tremble with fear.

The youngest son went to the pond and called on the frog to come to his rescue.

In a minute she was at his side, bringing with her the most lovely little dog, which she put into his arms. It sat up and begged with its paws, and went through the prettiest tricks, and was almost human in the way it understood and did what it was told.

In high spirits the youth carried it off to his mother. As soon as she saw it, she exclaimed: "This is the most beautiful little dog I have ever seen. You are indeed fortunate, my son, you have won a pearl of a wife."

Then, turning to all three, she said: "Here are three shirts. Take them to your chosen wives. Whoever sews the best will be my favourite daughter-in-law."

So the young men set out once more, and again, this time, the work of the frog was much the best and the neatest.

This time the mother said: "Now that I am

content with the tests I gave, I want you to go and fetch home your brides, and I will prepare the wedding-feast."

You may imagine what the youngest brother felt on hearing these words. Whence was he to fetch a bride? Would the frog be able to help him in this new difficulty? With bowed head, and feeling very sad, he sat down on the edge of the pond.

Flop! And once more the faithful frog was beside him. "What is troubling you?" she asked him, and then the youth told her everything. "Will you take me for a wife?" she asked.

"What should I do with you as a wife?" he replied, wondering at her strange proposal.

At this the frog disappeared. The next minute the youth beheld a lovely little chariot, drawn by two tiny ponies, standing on the road. The frog was holding the carriage door open for him to step in. "Come with me," she said. And he got up and followed her into the chariot.

As they drove along the road they met three witches. The first of them was blind, the second was hunchbacked, and the third had a large thorn in her throat. When the three witches beheld the chariot,

with the frog seated pompously among the cushions, they broke into such fits of laughter that the eyelids of the blind one burst open, and she recovered her sight, the hunchback rolled about on the ground in merriment till her back became straight, and in a roar of laughter the thorn fell out of the throat of the third witch. Their first thought was to reward the frog, who had unconsciously been the means of curing them of their misfortunes.

The first witch waved her wand over the frog, and changed her into the loveliest girl that had ever been seen. The second witch waved the wand over the tiny chariot and ponies, and they were turned into a beautiful large carriage with prancing horses, and a coachman on the seat. The third witch gave the girl a magic purse, filled with money. Having done this, the witches disappeared, and the youth with his lovely bride drove to his mother's home.

Great was the delight of the mother at her youngest son's good fortune. A beautiful house was built for them, she was the favourite daughter-in-law, and they lived happily ever after.

The Half-Chick

From Andrew Lang's *Green Fairy Book*

ONCE UPON A TIME there was a handsome black Spanish hen, who had a large brood of chickens. They were all fine, plump little birds, except the youngest. When he first chipped his shell his mother could scarcely believe her eyes, he was so different from the twelve

34

other downy, soft little chicks. This one looked as if he had been cut in two. He had only one leg, and one wing, and one eye, and he had half a head and half a beak. His mother shook her head sadly and said: "My youngest born can never grow up tall and handsome like his brothers. They will go out into the world and rule over poultry yards of their own, but this poor little fellow will always have to stay at home with his mother." And she called him Medio Pollito, which is Spanish for half-chick.

Now though Medio Pollito was such an odd, helpless-looking little thing, his mother soon found that he was not at all willing to remain under her wing and protection. Medio Pollito had a roving spirit in spite of his one leg, and as he grew older he became more self-willed and disobedient.

One day, he strutted up to his mother with the peculiar little hop and kick which was his way of walking, and cocking his one eye at her in a very bold way he said: "Mother, I am tired of this life in a dull farmyard, with nothing but a dreary maize field to look at. I'm off to Madrid to see the king."

"To Madrid, Medio Pollito!" exclaimed his mother. "Why, you silly chick, it would be a long journey for a grown-up cock, and a poor little thing like you would be tired out before you had gone half the distance. No, no, stay at home with your mother, and some day, when you are bigger, we will go on a little journey together."

But Medio Pollito had made up his mind.

"What is the use of our all crowding each other up in this poky little place?" he said. "When I have a fine courtyard of my own at the king's palace, I shall perhaps ask some of you to pay me a short visit," and scarcely waiting to say goodbye to his family, away he stumped down the high road that led to Madrid.

Later in the day, as he was taking a short cut through a field, he passed a stream. It was all choked up, and overgrown with weeds and water-plants, so that its waters could not flow freely.

"Oh! Medio Pollito," it cried, as the half-chick hopped along its banks, "do come and help me by clearing away these weeds."

"Help you, indeed!" exclaimed Medio Pollito. "Do you think I have nothing to do but to waste my time on such trifles? I am off to Madrid to see the king," and hoppity-kick, hoppity-kick, away stumped Medio Pollito.

A little later he came to a fire that had been left by some gipsies in a wood. It was burning very low.

"Oh! Medio Pollito," cried the fire, in a weak, wavering voice, "in a few minutes I shall go quite out, unless you put some sticks and dry leaves upon me. Do help me, or I shall die!"

"Help you, indeed!" answered Medio Pollito. "I have other things to do. I am off to Madrid to see the king," and hoppity-kick, hoppity-kick, away stumped Medio Pollito.

The next morning, as he was getting near Madrid, he passed a chestnut tree, in whose branches the wind was entangled. "Oh! Medio Pollito," called the wind, "do hop up here, and help me to get free."

"It is your own fault for going there," answered Medio Pollito. "I can't waste all my morning stopping here to help you, for I am off to Madrid to see the king," and hoppity-kick, hoppity-kick, away stumped Medio Pollito in great glee, for the towers and roofs of Madrid were now in sight.

When he entered the town he saw the king's palace, and he determined to hop up to the front gate and wait until the king came out. But as he was hopping past one of the back windows the king's cook saw him. "Here is the very thing I want," he exclaimed, "for the king has just sent a message to say that he must have chicken broth for his dinner," and opening the window he stretched out his arm, caught Medio Pollito, and popped him into the broth-pot that was standing near the fire. How wet and clammy the water felt as it went over Medio Pollito's head, making his feathers cling to his side.

"Water!" he cried. "Do not wet me like this."

"Ah! Medio Pollito," replied the water, "you would not help me when I was a little stream away on the fields, now you must be punished."

Then the fire began to burn and scald Medio Pollito, and he danced and hopped from one side of the pot to the other, and crying out in pain: "Fire! Do not scorch me like this!"

"Ah! Medio Pollito," answered the fire. "You would not help me when I was dying away in the wood. You are being punished."

Then the cook lifted up the lid of the pot to see if the broth was ready for the king's dinner.

"Look here!" he cried in horror. "This chicken is burned to a cinder. I can't send it to the royal table." He threw Medio Pollito into the street. But the wind caught him and whirled him through the air.

"Oh, wind!" he gasped out. "If you hurry me along like this you will kill me. Do let me rest a moment."

"Ah! Medio Pollito," replied the wind, "when I was caught in the branches of the chestnut tree you would not help me. Now you are punished." And he swirled Medio Pollito over the roofs of the houses till they reached the highest church, and there he left him fastened to the top of the steeple.

And there stands Medio Pollito to this day. And if you go to Madrid, and walk through the streets till you come to the highest church, you will see Medio Pollito perched on his one leg on the steeple, with his one wing drooping at his side, and gazing sadly out of his one eye over the town.